DEDICATION

To Susie Shellenberger and Pat Binder—
for all their help in bringing
The Cafeteria Lady to life . . . and
for always being willing to sample
my cooking. (They're both true people
of faith!)

the **cafeteria** lady

On the Loose

Martha Bolton

FOCUS ON THE FAMILY

PUBLISHING

Colorado Springs, Colorado

Library of Congress Cataloging-in-Publication Data
Bolton, Martha, 1951-
    On the loose : the cafeteria lady / by Martha Bolton.
        p.   cm.
    ISBN 1-56179-280-2
    1. High school students—Juvenile humor.   2. Girls—Juvenile humor.   3. Wit and
humor, Juvenile.   [1. High schools—Wit and humor.   2. Girls—Wit and humor.   3. Wit
and humor.   4. Schools—Wit and humor.]   I. Title.
PN6162.B635   1994
814'.54—dc20
                                                                                94-16857
                                                                                    CIP
                                                                                    AC

Published by Focus on the Family Publishing, Colorado Springs, Colorado 80995.
Distributed by Word Books, Dallas, Texas.

Editor: Lynn Rhoades
Designer: Jeff Stoddard

Printed in the United States of America
94 95 96 97 98 99/10 9 8 7 6 5 4 3 2 1

CONTENTS

ACKNOWLEDGMENTS

Thanks to:

My husband, Russ, who claims the recent 6.8 Los Angeles earthquake shook a few things into place at our house.

My sons, Russ II, Matt, and Tony, who, as mere infants, crawled into the kitchen and uttered their very first words, "Why is it so smoky in here?"

"The Regulators" youth group (they know who they are) for being such a terrific and fun group of teens.

To Al Janssen, Gwen Weising, and everyone at Focus on the Family Books for all their encouragement.

Finally, to Brio readers everywhere. I can't tell you how much I appreciate the wonderful letters you've written! And don't worry, those homemade brownies I promised each of you will be arriving shortly. I'm just waiting to take them out of my oven. Ummm . . . that crane should have been here hours ago!

FOREWORD

I've known Martha Bolton for over 65 years now. She and I grew up in a poor part of the country. We looked at ghettos and dreamed of one day moving there. Where we come from prairie dogs aren't wild animals, they're a side dish.

At one time it was one of the most beautiful parts of the country, with green grassy knolls, tall pine trees, and babbling brooks. Then, one day Martha decided to cook. Martha was unique. While every other girl in our neighborhood weighed about 350 pounds and smelled like Aunt Bea, Martha's dumplings weighed 350 pounds and smelled like Aunt Bea after she'd mowed the grass . . . in 103 degree heat!

Okay, so 65 years was an exaggeration. I've really known Martha for only about 9 years. (It's just felt like 65!) When Martha asked me to write the foreword for her new book, I wondered what could I say about Martha that could be printed. Well, first of all, if you've read any of her magazine columns, newspaper columns, or books, you already know Martha is a very funny lady. But she's more than that. She's the mother of three boys, the wife of one husband, and a committed Christian. She also helps lead the youth group at her church in Southern California. (I just hope she's not in charge of making the refreshments!)

I have appreciated watching Martha have a positive effect on the secular entertainment world. Martha is one of Bob Hope's full-time comedy writers. She has also written for Phyllis Diller,

Ann Jillian, and numerous other entertainers. She has done this without compromising her integrity or Christian witness. She's even let me have some of her leftover jokes (at a discounted price, of course) and for that I am truly grateful . . . as is my accountant. Martha is one of those Christians who believes in hauling the water to the desert—not just the ocean—touching her world, using her gift of humor to glorify the Creator of laughter. Write on, Martha, write on . . .

Mark Lowry

chapter one

a story with a **twist**

To this day I don't understand why I didn't make my high school gymnastics team. I had incredible strength in my upper arms—thanks to two semesters of lifting my homemade biscuits in Foods class. I had a natural sense of balance, too—if I padded myself with three pillows on my left side, I always padded myself with three pillows on my right side as well. So, why didn't I make the team? I asked our gymnastics coach that very same question.

"I just don't think gymnastics is your sport," she explained one day during floor exercises.

"Not my sport?" I protested. "What about all those cartwheels and somersaults I just did?"

She shook her head. "Sorry, but tripping on your way back to your seat doesn't count."

I wasn't about to give up on my gymnastic career that easily, so I pressed on.

"Don't you realize," I pointed out, "that I hold the school record for most time spent on the uneven parallel bars?"

"You hung a hammock between them and took a nap," she snapped.

As you can see, she was one tough coach. I really wanted to be on the team, though, so I gathered my courage and asked, "Coach, what exactly is it that I'm doing wrong?"

"Well," she began, "for one thing, your movements are too guarded."

"Too guarded?"

She nodded. "Maybe you haven't noticed, but you're the only one who wears a seatbelt on the balance beam. And you need to work on your dismount, too."

"What's wrong with the one I'm using now?"

"You mean the one where you sit on the horizontal bar and yell, 'Get me down from here! Get me down from here'?"

"It's original," I smiled.

Without hesitation, she continued her critique.

"And you don't seem very flexible."

"Are you kidding?" I said. "I'm as flexible as they come. If I don't get to practice my routine today, then I'll practice it tomorrow or next week or next month."

"I was referring to your muscular flexibility."

"My muscles are very flexible," I insisted. "I can get them to sag either to the left or to the right. And you have to admit my timing's good."

"Yes," she nodded, "you have perfect timing. You only do your routine when an ambulance is in the immediate area."

"So, are you going to put me on the team?" I pressed.

She shook her head. "But don't let it get you down. We took some pictures of a few of your landings—you know, where your legs ended up wrapped around your neck and your shoulders switched sides."

"Ah, yes, my better ones. And . . . ?"

"Well, I have a feeling those pictures might open up a whole new career for you."

"Really?" I exclaimed. "As a gymnast?"

"No," she said. "But I hear a cracker company is looking for a new pretzel pattern."

chapter two

don't **wake** me 'til after lunch!

Wouldn't you like to meet the man or woman who decided school should start in the A.M.? I mean, what kind of person enjoys watching half-awake teenagers show up to class wearing one Reebok and one armadillo bedroom slipper? Does this individual find it amusing when a sleepy-eyed eighth-grader inadvertently starts doing her math assignment with a mascara wand? Or when a drowsy ninth-grader tries sharpening his pencil in the drinking fountain?

I've long felt there would be tremendous advantages to beginning school later in the day. For one thing, a late afternoon history class would be better, because by then there'd be a little more history to study. And evening P.E. classes would be far more popular. In the dark, no one would worry about how they looked in their gym clothes.

Personally, I could have used a later beginning bell when I went to school. You see, I was always a late sleeper. Some mornings the only way to get me out of bed was to put helium in my pajamas. Okay, once I did happen to get up for school on time, but hey, I couldn't count on an earthquake striking *every* morning.

My folks tried to get me to use an alarm clock, but I could never find one I liked. They all made noise when they went off and would wake me up.

But somehow, I always managed to get up, dress, and drag myself to school. I wasn't fully awake until well after noon, though, so my morning classes suffered. The only thing my first-period Spanish class taught me was how to snore in two languages. And I barely passed my second-period sewing class. That's because while everyone else was making blouses, skirts, jumpsuits, and gym bags, all I wanted to make was a pillow.

My third-period English class didn't fare much better. My oral report on someone who had inspired my life only rated a "D." My teacher didn't think Rip van Winkle was a good choice for a role model.

So, I had to adjust. I had to face the fact that school wasn't for the sleepy-headed. The school board was never going to issue desk chairs that recline or allow lullabies to be played over the P.A. It was high time I woke up and realized the sink in Foods class was no place to catch my zzz's.

If I wanted an education, I had to get it like everyone else— awake. So, that's what I did. And to this day, I can still remember those touching words that my mother said to my father when I finally brought home my diploma. Beaming with pride, she looked into my wide-open eyes, then turned to my dad and said, "See, I told you they were blue!"

chapter three

the sweet taste of **success**

I saw it with my own eyes, but I still couldn't believe it: my teacher was giving every student in my homeroom a box of 30 candy bars. Thirty giant bars of delicious, creamy milk chocolate! Was I dreaming in class . . . again?

I raised my hand. "Mmphfrumphonimonf?" I asked, scarfing down the first bar.

She didn't understand a single word I said. Being quite used to that, she merely continued her mysterious distribution.

Licking the remaining crumbs of the second bar from my fingers, I swallowed and repeated my question.

"This is really nice of you," I smiled. "But, why?"

You see, nice was not the sort of behavior this teacher was known for. Most of the teachers I had throughout my school years were okay, but this particular one was known around campus as Attila the Hun of the educational system. She gave growling lessons to pit bulls. She also gave out some of the longest detentions known to man. (One of my classmates is still serving his.) So, why the sudden generosity?

Snatching the third bar from my mouth (and removing three of my fillings along with it), she snapped, "They're not for you to eat. You're supposed to sell them."

"Sell them," I said, the words whistling through the newly exposed holes in my teeth.

"That's right," my teacher stated firmly. "It's a fund-raiser for additional classroom equipment." (She must've seen a stun gun on sale.)

Okay, I thought to myself, *how difficult can it be to sell 30 candy bars? No one can say no to chocolate, right?*

The first 48 people I approached said no to chocolate. I had to eat three more bars just to get over the rejection.

I wasn't ready to give up yet. I tried my relatives next, figuring that being related to me was surely worth a dollar candy bar.

It wasn't. Aunt Ruth was on a diet. Uncle Henry was watching his cholesterol. My parents said they were cutting down on their sugar intake. And my sisters had their own boxes to sell for their class.

"I'm getting nowhere fast," I grumbled, polishing off two more bars out of sheer frustration.

That night, I consumed four more bars while making a list of who I'd try selling to the following day. I shouldn't have bothered. I don't know how they managed, but by ten o'clock the next morning, my sisters had beaten me to everyone on my list. Had it not been for the six additional candy bars I ate, I really would've felt terrible.

It was time to revamp my marketing strategy. But 12 candy bars later, the only thing I had revamped was my figure. I had put on an additional four pounds. It didn't matter by then, though, because my box was finally empty.

That wasn't so bad, I said to myself. Maybe I should try selling another box. After all, my teacher was awarding a prize to the top-selling student in the class. Maybe . . . just maybe it'd be me.

I couldn't wait to check out my second box. Then, my third. Then, my fourth. There was no stopping me now. By the time the fund-raiser was over, I was clearly the winner. No one else even came close.

Sure, I'd eaten all the candy myself, but hey, that pocket comb I won was worth every last dime of the $120 I now owed the school.

But more importantly, my impressive salesmanship even made my teacher smile . . . which was kind of nice, because until then I had no idea she had such a pretty tooth.

chapter four

toast encounters of the **burnt** kind

Anyone who has ever tasted my cooking knows that I failed Foods class. Okay, I didn't actually fail. I merely got transferred to Wood Shop. They figured my recipes would go over better there. The theory? If my meat loaf turned out inedible, at least I could make bookends out of it.

I have to say, before the transfer, I actually enjoyed Foods. I learned a lot of important things in that class, too. I learned gelatin shouldn't take three weeks to gel, steak shouldn't be as tough as sheet metal, and cookies shouldn't make the oven rack sag when you bake them.

The most difficult class recipe for me to prepare was a dish called "egg à la king." I'm not saying how my version turned out, but those students who were brave enough to try it spent so much time in the nurse's office, they could have qualified for a medical degree.

I still counted on getting a good grade on that assignment because the teacher took so much time sampling mine. I figured she wanted to savor every morsel. As it turned out, the eggshells were slowing down her chewing.

Learning about nutrition was a major part of Foods class. I discovered that proper eating habits can actually prolong one's life. Or, to put it another way, I should never eat my own cooking.

Foods class also taught me about the four different food groups: the meat and bean group, the fruit and vegetable group, the bread and cereal group, and the brownie and hot fudge sundae group. (Or was that the cheesecake and banana split group?)

I also learned the proper use of various kitchen utensils. I learned butter knives were for butter, bread knives were for bread, and electric Skil-saws were for my pineapple upside-down cakes.

I learned how to operate, care for, and appreciate what has since become the most valuable and trusted tool in my kitchen today—the can opener.

My teacher taught us how to use a timer, too. A timer lets me know exactly when a dish is done, and it's much quieter than the smoke alarm.

Foods class also taught me how to set a table. But I still can't remember if the stomach pump goes on the right side or the left side of the plate.

Yes, looking back, I'd have to say I had a great time in Foods. And even though my time in the class was limited, it did have its advantages. Just think of all the extra fire drills the school had because of me!

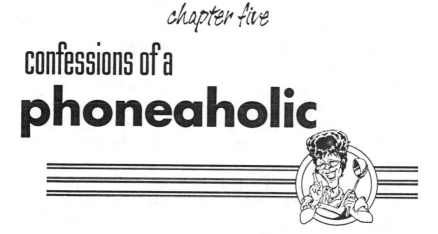

chapter five

confessions of a
phoneaholic

Do you spend a lot of time on the telephone? Did you do your last term paper on the yellow pages? Does your monthly telephone bill come to your house by UPS . . . in two trucks? Is your favorite tune the dial tone? Does the operator know you by your first name and send you a Christmas card every year?

If you answered "yes" to any of the above, then we have something in common. I, too, am a phoneaholic. My case is so severe that twice last year my family had to call the rescue unit to untangle me from the phone cord.

I have it bad. Whenever I go to a beauty salon, I have my hair styled around my receiver. I've got blisters on my index fingers from pushing telephone buttons. And now, my doctor's talking about doing skin grafts to repair the wear and tear on my ears.

The problem dates back to my childhood. The very first words I ever uttered were "Is it for me?"

As a teen, the situation only worsened. The telephone and I became inseparable. I went to bed with it next to me. I woke up with it next to me. At mealtime, it was part of my place setting.

My parents tried numerous times to get me to give up the telephone because my habit was affecting the family. I remember relatives complaining once that they had tried calling our line all summer and could only get a busy signal. They were mistaken, though. Okay, I'll admit to August, but I know I hung up twice in July.

My love for the telephone also affected our vacations. My family didn't think it was much fun limiting travel to only as far as the cord could reach.

Teens today don't have to worry about things like that. There are cordless phones. There's also "call waiting." We didn't have call waiting when I was a teen. We only had "Dad waiting." You knew another call might be trying to get through by how fast his foot was tapping on the floor next to you.

We didn't have "conference calling" either. The only time three people were on the same line was when my big sister was eavesdropping.

I could go on about my lifelong affliction with the telephone. I could describe how my heart starts to palpitate and I break out into a cold sweat every time I see a phone commercial on television.

I could confess that I've worn finger grooves in my telephone receiver from years of extended usage.

I could also tell you about the flowers the phone company sent me last month for being such a loyal customer.

Then, there are the recurring nightmares—you know, the ones about storms and downed telephone lines.

Yes, I could tell you about all that, but it's time to bring this chapter to a close now. I think I hear my phone ringing . . .

chapter six

fuzzy bread, jelly beans,
and **ant condos**

June usually means it's time to clear out your locker. But if you keep your locker as clean as I kept mine, you probably won't be done until sometime in August.

You wouldn't believe some of the things I used to discover buried in my locker. Things like six pairs of old gym socks. I'm not saying what they smelled like, but if Los Angeles would hang up just one of them, they'd never again have a Med fly problem.

Then, there was that library book I thought I'd lost. Sure, the fine was a little stiff (especially since the due date was BC), but at least I could now return it.

I also discovered numerous mysterious food items—petrified gum, a jelly bean with hair growing out of it, and a cupcake that was doubling as some sort of ant condo. And how could I forget that egg salad sandwich on green, fuzzy bread whose odor had already prompted two school evacuations?

Then, there were all those missing homework assignments I had unjustly accused my dog of devouring. But I should have known he didn't eat them. He always preferred my report cards.

I also unearthed numerous school supplies—pens, pencils, erasers, rulers, paper clips—you know, all the things I was supposed to bring to class but could never find.

My school picture was buried in there, too. Of course, considering how it turned out, it was better off staying buried.

Next came notes from my friends to me, notes from me to my friends, and notes from my teacher telling us to quit writing notes.

My extra gym shorts, which I had fully intended to take home and wash sometime during the year, were also in there. By that time, though, they could walk home by themselves.

I also found my winter jacket—the one I'd spent all winter looking for, along with numerous sweaters, wallets, and make-up pouches that I had, in a panic, reported to the lost-and-found department throughout the year.

I could always count on finding several dollars in loose change, as well as numerous buttons, earrings, and lipsticks that had melted from locker heat and now looked like the Leaning Tower of Pisa.

This was all in addition to outdated field trip permission slips, old fund-raiser packets, notebooks, brushes, enough paper to rewrite my history book, my spare locker key (*inside* my locker), two mirrors, and a partridge in a pear tree.

With so much stuff crammed into my locker, no wonder I was always the last student to leave campus on the final day of school. But the principal couldn't complain. Like I told him, I could have cleaned out my locker a lot faster if he had only let me bring that moving van on campus.

chapter seven

nobody knows the **troubles** I've sewn

Okay, so maybe sewing wasn't my best subject in school. Maybe I *did* deserve a "D" on that blouse I made with all the fringe . . . especially since it wasn't supposed to have any. I couldn't help it—the scissors just kept slipping.

Perhaps the teacher had a right to take points off for the way I hemmed it, too. But I still say the staples didn't show *that* much. She may have even had a point when she told me one sleeve per side would have been plenty.

Still, no one can say I didn't try. I put forth a lot of effort in that class! I became an expert on all the basic stitches: the running stitch, the basting stitch, the backstitch, even the ones the doctor used in the emergency room when I accidentally sewed my thumb to my gym bag.

I taught myself the fastest way to thread a needle, too. You just lick the end of the thread, miss the eye of the needle 14 times, then ask the kid next to you to do it.

The zigzag button on the sewing machine was another skill I mastered. I seldom needed it, though, since most of my stitches came out zigzagged anyway.

I also learned the easiest way to let out a seam—eat too many desserts in the school cafeteria.

And, if satisfied customers are the mark of a good seamstress, I had that sewn up as well. My family was proud to wear each and every item I sewed for them. They must have been. They were always popping their buttons.

So then, why didn't I pass the class?

Looking back now, one of the main reasons was probably due to my many safety violations. I didn't mean to be, but I was a real danger to myself in that class. I stuck my fingers with the needle so many times, I looked like I had arm-wrestled a porcupine. No wonder my teacher made me wear a full-body thimble.

I always had to stay twenty minutes after class, too. Not because the teacher made me . . . it just took that long to untangle myself from all the thread.

I'm sure I posed a safety threat to fellow students as well. Why else would the school insurance policy require the room be evacuated before I was allowed to cut out patterns?

The major factor in my poor grade, though, had to have been my year-end project. It was worth a total of 500 points, but my teacher refused to give me *any* credit at all. She said it wasn't that it didn't display incredible sewing talent. It did. The seams were perfect, the hem was exceptional, and the collar didn't pop up and knock the wearer unconscious like the one on my last project did.

"It's terrific," my teacher explained, handing it back to me. "But if you're going to turn in something this good, you should remember one thing."

"What's that?" I asked, beaming with pride.

"Always remove the J.C. Penney's tag first."

chapter eight

it's a **snap!**

You know when school picture day arrives. That's the morning you wake up with a pimple the size of Mount Everest on your forehead. (You know it's big when your best friend asks to hang her jacket on it!)

The only thing you can do with a pimple this enormous is to apply Clearasil with a paint roller and hope for the best. After all, you certainly can't pop it. You need special clearance to pop a pimple this big—you know, so you won't accidentally shoot down aircraft.

Another sign that school picture day is here is the wind. For some unknown reason, the wind always seems to blow its hardest on school picture day. You can spend hours combing, gelling, spraying, and spritzing, but take one step outside and your hair will look as if it was styled at "Coiffures by Cyclones."

Sometimes it even rains on picture day. It rained so hard on my ninth-grade picture day, if you look closely at the finished photo, you can see our principal in the background gathering animals two by two.

There's an unwritten rule that picture day will also be scheduled during the worst part of the allergy season—when your nose is red and your eyes are itchy. Usually, though, the photographer will be understanding and won't snap the picture until you're in the middle of a good sneeze.

Most of my school pictures turned out less than flattering. My eyes had that "rested" look . . . they were closed. And I was never very happy with my smile. Either it was too broad (my dentist could use the photo for my annual cavity checkup), or I didn't smile at all (as in when picture day and report card day occur at the same time).

Trying to get the right smile out of me was often a problem. I remember one photographer who kept saying "Cheese! Cheese!" I thought he wanted me to repeat the word so he could catch a good smile. He was merely pointing out that I had some Velveeta on my chin.

Another problem with my school pictures was something called "The Home Permanent Syndrome." My mother always insisted on giving me a home permanent the week before the photo session. These weren't the same home permanents that are available today, however. The '90s teenager is lucky. She can choose between body perms, soft perms, and curly perms.

In my day, we only had one choice—the electric shock perm. After one of those babies, your hair didn't just curl. It exploded. It stood on its ends and pointed in more directions than a broken compass. That's why they were called "home" permanents. After you got one, you never wanted to leave home!

But even if my school pictures didn't turn out so well, I'm still glad I have them. After all these years, it's fun to see how fashions and hairstyles have changed. And when I display them in just the right places, they really do keep the snails out of my garden.

chapter nine

greetings
from camp itchiskin

I remember my first camp. Eight girls from my church registered to go. We went in two cars and a 30-foot bus. The bus was for our luggage. It had to make two trips.

Surely our pastor didn't expect us to leave behind such life-or-death necessities as blow-dryers, curling irons, makeup mirrors, manicure sets, and our entire summer wardrobes. Just because we were roughing it didn't mean we shouldn't look good. The point was to get in touch with nature, not scare it away.

Once at the camp, we were assigned a cabin and given a quick rundown of what was offered. The best was horseback riding. We could ride as long as we wanted, providing the horse was plugged in and we didn't run out of quarters. (Okay, so it was a budget camp.)

Most camps have daily schedules. Ours did, too. It was:

6:30	Wake-up call played by bugle boy at camp flagpole.
6:40	Second wake-up call played by bugle boy at cabin door of any campers still asleep.
6:50	Final wake-up call played by bugle boy into ear of any camper still asleep.
7:00	Breakfast
7:30	Pepto-Bismol distribution
9:00	Chapel
11:00	Free time
11:01	Group activities
12:00	Lunch
12:30	Rolaids distribution
1:00	Free time
1:01	Crafts and sports
5:00	Dinner
5:30	Tums distribution
7:00	Chapel
10:00	Lights out in cabins

That last item on the schedule was the hardest for our cabin to comply with. Not that our counselor didn't try. It's just that with our group, "lights out" usually went something like this:

10:00	Lights out
10:01	Lights on as camp counselor screams and wants to know who put the ice cubes in her sleeping bag.
10:03	Lights out again
10:04	Lights on as counselor discovers rubber snake under her pillow.
10:06	Lights out again
10:07	Lights on as a mysterious scratching noise is heard at cabin window.
10:08	Counselor assures campers that it's probably just the wind. The bear seen earlier that day eating from the cafeteria trash can was surely too sick by now to bother anybody.
10:09	Lights out
10:10	Lights on as campers express their hunger and wonder if the camp offers room service.

This routine continued throughout the night. In fact, our lights went on and off so many times, I'm surprised aircraft didn't think we were signaling them to try to land.

All in all, though, my memories of camp are fond ones. It was good to get away with other Christian teens for a week of fun and learning. And to tell you the truth, we were having such a good time, we even forgot to get homesick.

No, I take that back. One of us *did* cry and beg to go home. But we all told our counselor just to hang in there. Camp would be over before she knew it.

chapter ten

two, four, six, **nine**——who's that cheering out of time?

In high school, my dream was to become a majorette. After all, how difficult could it be to master the art of baton twirling? You just spin the baton around in your fingers, toss it into the air, and wait for it to come down. Unfortunately, at the tryouts, mine came down on top of the judge's head . . . 14 times. For some nit-picking reason, this cost me points and I wasn't selected.

My next choice was the drill team. Even though it was the

same judge (I recognized the ice pack), I thought I had a fair shot at making the team. How hard could it be simply to march in formation?

I soon found out. The tryouts were held on the football field, and our test was to march together, ultimately forming a map of the United States. At first, that didn't seem difficult. I just followed everyone else. When they turned left, I turned left. When they turned right, I turned right. I soon got the distinct feeling I'd done something wrong, though, when I ended up in the parking lot . . . alone. I tried to convince the judge I was one of the Hawaiian Islands and was supposed to be that far from the mainland. She didn't buy it.

I had to admit formation marching wasn't for me. Still, I wasn't about to give up. I persuaded the judge to consider me as one of the school banner carriers. Surely, carrying the banner ahead of our drill team would be a piece of cake. I ended up looking more like a jelly roll, though, after I got tangled up in the banner and had to be rolled off the field.

After that, I decided to give cheerleading a try. The competition was even tougher. The other girls screamed a lot louder and jumped a lot higher than I did—especially every time I accidentally stepped on their toes.

The hardest part of the cheerleader tryouts was when I had to climb on the shoulders of five other girls and form a human pyramid. I made it, but two of the girls filed a complaint because I had used their faces as steps. I tried to deny it, but my shoe prints were still fresh in their makeup. Needless to say, I didn't pass the cheerleading tryouts, either.

Now, there was only one way to show my school spirit—as a fan. But not just *any* fan. I determined I was going to be the best fan our school had ever seen! I cheered. I screamed. I got so many waves going, half the audience got seasick. Most of all, I had fun. I also discovered something. I discovered the fans in the stands are just as important as the majorettes, the drill team, the cheerleaders, and even the football team.

Speaking of the football team, they appreciated my cheering, too. I know that because after their last game of the season, the entire team grabbed me and tossed me up in the air. Sure, this was something they did on a regular basis throughout the school year, but this time it was different. *This* time they stuck around to catch me when I came back down.

chapter eleven

what a **chore!**

If you're like most teens, you have chores to do—chores that only grow bigger the longer you put them off. Having found this out the hard way, I can now offer the following tips. You know you're behind on your chores when . . .

- The last clean newspaper in the bottom of your parrot's cage is dated BC.
- You haven't given your dog a bath for so long, the only

thing he'll sit up and beg for is some deodorant.

- You can't remember the last time you cleaned your pool, but you don't recall it having all those alligators before.
- Buzzards are circling your overflowing trash cans . . . the ones *inside* the house.
- Your mountain of dirty laundry is so high you could ski down it.
- There's so much dirt on your kitchen floor you don't know whether to call Mr. Clean or an archaeologist.
- The house plants you forgot to water are dead, but the ones sprouting in the living room carpeting are thriving.
- There's so much dust on your furniture even the flies are wheezing.
- Tourists mistake that pile of dirty dishes in your sink for the Washington Monument.
- You discover things under your bed that even Ripley wouldn't believe.
- Your closet is so cluttered, the moths need special clearance to land.
- You haven't mowed your front yard for so long, the overgrown grass has swallowed a month's worth of newspapers, two paper boys, and the mailman.
- But you really know you're behind on your chores when you open your refrigerator door and a four-month-old chicken salad sandwich climbs out and walks itself to the garbage disposal.

chapter twelve
it's my night to **cook**
—where'd everybody go?

When I was a teen, Tuesdays were my night to cook. Coincidentally, my family spent a lot of Wednesdays sick in bed. You've heard of Wolfgang Puk? I was known as the Wolfgang Yuck of the kitchen.

It wasn't that I didn't try. Every Tuesday I'd prepare a full seven-course meal for each member of my family. It usually consisted of soup, salad, the main entrée, vegetable, dessert, and two Rolaids. But did anyone appreciate it? No. All I ever heard were complaints:

"There's a worm in my salad."

"I just shattered a molar on this biscuit."

"I think your pot roast is eating its way through my plate."

Picky, picky, picky. Instead of letting their comments get me down, though, I merely determined to try that much harder. On several occasions I even went to the trouble of preparing appetizers. Unfortunately, this didn't impress them, either. No one liked my crab cakes. (I don't know why. I put frosting on them and everything.) And the only positive thing they had to say about my cheese ball was that it was great for slam-dunking.

My main courses went equally unappreciated. Everyone said my rack of lamb tasted more like a rack than a lamb. One night, they also voted to rename my brisket of beef, "risk it of beef."

My desserts were ridiculed as well. No one ever touched my sponge cake. (And that's after I told them I used only new sponges in the recipe.) My Tower of Babel gelatin mold wasn't a family favorite, either. (I called it that because it was multi-tiered, and no one could ever finish it.)

One good thing about my Tuesday-night dinners was that they were always well-balanced. I'm not talking nutritionally, of course. I'm strictly referring to weight distribution. Not once did I place my meat loaf on the same side of the table as my muffins. I knew if I did that, the table would tip over.

I also deserve credit for all those times I had to improvise. If there wasn't any Velveeta in the house, I'd serve macaroni and Cheese-Its. No Spanish rice? No problem. I'd just serve salsa and Rice Krispies.

Yes, those Tuesday-night experiences were where I picked up all my kitchen know-how, my culinary creativity, my Doctorate of Indigestion. There, I learned to appreciate fine food. In other words, there I first realized the benefits of eating out.

chapter thirteen

cupid's **big** challenge

As a teenager, I didn't date all that much. Oh, I had plenty of cute guys asking for my telephone number, but it was usually after I'd backed into their cars in parking lots. The boys at my school were always chasing after me, too. That is, until the principal finally put a stop to it. He made me quit taking their lunch trays.

My friends tried their best to nudge my love life along by

setting me up with blind dates. After going on a few of these, though, I began to have serious doubts about their friendship.

First, there was the boy who insisted on bringing his pet along on our date. Normally, I wouldn't have minded, but did he have to give that ostrich the *front* seat?

Then, there was "Mr. Gorgeous." That wasn't my nickname for him. It was his. All he did for the entire date was look into my eyes. I was flattered till I realized he was just checking out his hair in the reflection.

My most embarrassing date was the guy who kept saying he could tell I was into health foods. I assumed he was commenting on my muscle tone and overall healthy appearance, so I flashed him the biggest smile I could. But he wasn't complimenting my health. He was merely pointing out that I had some spinach stuck between my teeth.

My worst blind date of all, though, was the guy whose breath was so bad that when he tried whispering a sweet nothing in my ear, he melted my earring!

One reason boys didn't ask me out on their own was the fact that I was a terrible flirt. I don't mean I flirted a lot. I mean I was a *terrible* flirt. I batted my eyelashes at a guy for five minutes once, but all he did was walk over, hand me a piece of paper, and walk away.

Confident it was a love note, I quickly opened it. Instead of poetry and words of love, it was simply the name of a doctor he thought could help me with my twitch.

The good news is that after years of dating disappointments and disasters, I finally did meet the love of my life. All the waiting was worth it. I was crazy about him and he fell head over heels for me. (I'm almost positive he would have done it, too, even if I hadn't tripped him!)

chapter fourteen

in the **swim** of things

I've never been very good at water athletics. Holding my breath is no problem. After all those years of opening my gym locker, I've perfected that skill.

It's just that I'm not a very good swimmer. I swim like a starfish. There are only two places you'll find me in a pool . . . at the bottom or clinging to the side. I'm the type of person who wears a life preserver in the shower (and even with that,

I've had to be rescued twice).

My attempt at waterskiing was pretty pathetic. I did a toe-hold front to back, then a helicopter, followed by a perfect toe-hold side slide, and that was just while trying to get my skis on. On the lake I wasn't much better. Sure, I brought the skis up out of the water on my first try, but unfortunately, I was under them.

I gave surfing a try once. I thought I had done pretty well, too, until the lifeguard explained to me that "catching the curl" did not mean grabbing the ponytail of a nearby swimmer and holding on for dear life.

Snorkeling is lots of fun. Seeing fish and underwater life up close can be exciting. Every time I try it, though, all the water spills out of our aquarium.

Another popular water sport is high diving. Every summer I go to our local public pool to practice my technique. It's beginning to pay off, too, because last week I finally managed to execute a perfect triple somersault with a half-twist. Okay, I admit it would've been more spectacular if I'd hit the pool instead of the shrubbery, but even Olympic gold medalists had to start somewhere.

Anyway, public pools are just for fun, right? And I was having plenty of fun last week. That is, until one rude little girl started splashing water in my face. I put up with it for as long as I could, then finally told her to go play somewhere else and leave the steps for the adults.

But where else could she have gone? The pool was so crowded we had to take turns going under.

Considering the cramped conditions, I could understand why the pool rules had to be strictly enforced. There wasn't enough room for the swimmers, much less rafts, so I under-stood why the lifeguard made me quit diving with mine. I didn't even complain when he made me take off the goggles and inflatable ring. But he went entirely too far when he asked me to remove my frog feet.

I wasn't wearing any.

chapter fifteen

things that make you go **uh-oh!**

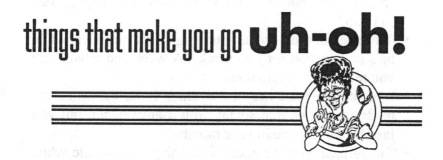

As a baby, my first word wasn't "Mama," "Dada," or "Triple Fudge Brownie Supreme." No, my very first utterance was "uh-oh."

Because of my vast talent for messing up, I can present you with this comprehensive list of *things that make you go uh-oh:*

- You mistake your brother's fungus experiment for a casserole and have two helpings.

- You catch the little boy you're baby-sitting on the telephone ordering pizza . . . from Italy.
- It's March 10 and you find a library book that was due on March 1 . . . four years ago.
- Just when you've applied a perm to your hair, wax to your legs, and a green herbal mask to your face, that cute new guy from school stops by to say "Hi."
- The meat loaf you mixed with your hands in Foods class turns out delicious. Later, though, you discover two of your acrylic fingernails are missing.
- You're in the church choir singing "Rock of Ages" the best you've ever sung it when the lady next to you discreetly points out that the rest of the choir is singing "Just as I Am."
- You remember to turn on your neighbor's sprinklers while he's on vacation for two weeks. A week and a half later you remember to turn them off.
- Your mother asks you not to touch those brownies she made for the church social. You'd answer her, but you just put the last one in your mouth.
- You surprise your brother by washing his favorite white shirt. It comes out clean, but you don't recall it having that pink hue and being two sizes too small for a Ken doll.
- After eating chili with onions, garlic bread, and a box of Milk Duds for lunch, you remember you have a dentist appointment after school.
- You stay up half the night studying for an exam on Chapter 9 in history class, only to find out the exam is on Chapter 10 . . . in English class.

- But what will really make you go "uh-oh!" is when you slip a bag of ice cubes, a rubber snake, and eight plastic spiders into your best friend's sleeping bag at camp. Then, just as you're awaiting her scream of shock and terror, you find out the camp counselor is borrowing her sleeping bag for the weekend!

chapter sixteen

taken for a **ride**

I love amusement parks! I love wild, scary rides that go up and down and 'round and 'round at breathtaking speeds. You know, the rides where you close your eyes, hang on with all your might, and scream for mercy . . . but enough about the merry-go-round.

Water rides are my *favorite*. I enjoy getting thoroughly drenched as I travel through waterfalls and down roaring rapids. I usually bring several changes of clothing for rides like this. It saves me a fortune at the Laundromat.

Roller coasters can be economical, too. After two corkscrew spirals, a vertical loop, and an 80-foot drop at 70 mph, I don't have to mousse my hair for a week.

Roller coasters can be frightening, though. I recall one that was so scary, the man in front of me couldn't stop his teeth from chattering. I know because they landed on my lap after the first upside-down loop.

The only ride I ever fainted on was a roller coaster. But it was nothing I could help. Whenever 30 sweaty people raise their arms at the same time, it's more than any human can bear.

One ride I can do without is the bumper cars. I don't see the point of zigzagging through traffic, swerving to miss the car to my left, bumping into the car to my right, then spinning around and driving in the opposite direction. I did all that on my driving test.

Standing in long lines is inevitable at most amusement parks, but there can be an advantage to this. Should you fall short of the height requirement for the ride, don't worry. Just go ahead and get in line. By the time your turn comes, chances are you'll have grown the necessary inches.

My favorite activity at an amusement park is to eat. And eat. And eat. And eat. Vendors see me coming and start sending out for backup. I love *all* the goodies . . . cotton candy, popcorn, pretzels, funnel cakes. (Those *are* the four food groups, aren't they?)

I eat from the moment I walk through the entrance gate until the park closes. I've discovered, though, that it's not a good idea to eat too many funnel cakes before riding the sky buckets.

It can be quite embarrassing when your bucket's hanging about ten feet lower than all the other buckets. All in all, I think amusement parks are terrific. And who really cares if you end the day weighing a few more pounds? By then your wallet has lost most of *its* weight, so it all evens out.

chapter seventeen

from **stretches** to stretchers

Over the years I've gotten a lot of use out of my collection of aerobics videos. I've found that if I stack 10 or 12 of them on top of each other, they make a great footstool.

My chief complaint with most aerobics videos is they're far too difficult to keep up with. I bought one the other day that has the instructor moving so fast, the only way I can keep pace is to put it on freeze-frame . . . and even then I have to take two breaks.

I don't understand how these exercise experts can make it look so easy. They go through their entire workout and barely sweat a drop. I, on the other hand, push the "play" button on my VCR and it's time to call 9-1-1.

Step exercises are popular right now, and I've been trying them. Every night on my way to the refrigerator I step over my rowing machine, step over my ski simulator, step over my barbells. It's fun, but I've yet to notice any real benefits.

Someone told me a trampoline provides a good workout. I bought one, and I have to admit it can really get me working up quite a sweat . . . especially when I fall asleep on it in the sun.

Don't get me wrong. I realize exercise is an important factor in maintaining good health. It's just that I've never committed myself to a regular fitness program. My idea of a warm-up exercise is popping a frozen pizza in the microwave, and the only cool-down exercise I do is chasing a Good Humor truck down the street.

This attitude is nothing new with me. Whenever I played hopscotch as a child, I drew only one square. I was even kicked off my high school tennis team. The coach didn't like me using the net as a hammock.

But I know there are others who are just like me. That's why I'm considering producing my own aerobics video: "The Cafeteria Lady—Gaspin' to the Oldies." It would offer creative ways to work out. For stretching exercises we'd have taffy pulls, and the only time we'd do knee bends is when we've dropped a Twinkie on the floor.

And forget weight lifting. My video would offer a better way to build those biceps. In time with the music, we'd attempt to open vacuum-sealed bags of potato chips. Not only is this a great workout for the upper arms, but jumping up and down on the impossible-to-open bag does wonders for thighs and calves, too. And pushing the detonator on the dynamite in that final attempt to open the bag works the forearm and stomach muscles as well.

I think the video would be a best-seller. If not? Well, I can always use a taller footstool.

chapter eighteen

little **class** of horrors

The only reason I enrolled in my high school's horticulture class was because all my friends said it would be an easy "A." NOT!

I *might* have gotten a good grade if my teacher had given me extra credit for the plants I was cultivating under my bed. But he refused. He would only count plants like carrots, corn, and green beans. I explained to him there was an excellent chance carrots, corn, and green beans *were* growing under my bed, but he still wouldn't budge.

He insisted that in order to pass his class, I had to do all my work in the horticulture field under his direct supervision. He had to actually see me tilling the soil, planting the plants, and nurturing them to maturity. I knew then I never should have listened to my friends. But there was no way out. I rolled up my sleeves and tried to be the best gardener I could be.

My first assignment was to plant bulbs. Unfortunately, I didn't receive a high score on this. It wasn't really my fault, though. My teacher hadn't specified which kind of bulbs to plant. I went with 60-watt bulbs. Obviously, I was wrong because when he saw it, he not only gave me an "F" on the assignment, but sent me to the principal's office as well.

I didn't do much better when it came to planting seeds. I made my furrows and rows (otherwise known as speed bumps for field mice), planted my seeds, watered them faithfully, and still, after six weeks of constant vigilance, the only thing I could see popping up through the soil was a gopher. And even he looked pretty embarrassed about the whole thing.

I didn't pass our avocado pit project either. Each student in the class had to put an avocado pit in a cup, place it on the windowsill, and wait for it to grow. Within weeks every one of my classmates' pits had sprouted roots and was growing nicely. Again, my pit did nothing. It sat there for two-and-a-half months, and all it got was a tan.

As you can see, when it comes to gardening, I'm all thumbs . . . and none of them are green. I've been known to drown seaweed and dehydrate a cactus. I've forgotten forget-me-nots and have given the weeping willow plenty to weep about. In fact,

I'm such a terrible gardener, the other night I thought I heard my Chia pet growling at me.

So, maybe I did deserve the poor grade my teacher gave me in horticulture class. But I still say he could have given me extra credit for the moss I'd been successfully growing in my gym locker all year!

chapter nineteen

look out, I'm on a roll!

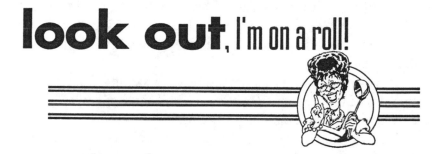

Don't get me wrong. I think roller skating is a great sport and a terrific form of exercise. There's no better way to burn off calories than falling down and getting back up again.

It's just that, well, maybe it's not the right sport for me. I have a hard time keeping my legs from tangling up when I *walk*, much less *skate*.

I came to this decision recently after winning a free skate

session at the local roller rink.

Upon entering the rink, the first thing I had to do was rent skates.

"Do you have a pair that'll fit me?" I asked.

"I doubt it," the man said, glancing at my feet. "But there may be a couple of guitar boxes in the trash bin next door that we could put some wheels on."

Sensing I wasn't amused, he handed me the largest pair he had in stock. "Godzilla only wore them once," he explained.

Taking the skates, I thanked him, then turned to find a place to sit down.

The only available seat was next to a guy whose odor-eaters had expired . . . four years ago. I held my breath, sat down, and began the challenge of lacing up. (Godzilla nothing! The shape those laces were in made me think they dated all the way back to Methuselah!)

It was a little scary stepping onto the skating floor for the first time in more than 10 years. And all those show-offs who actually *stayed up* didn't help my ego.

Determined to give it my best shot, I boldly began. To my surprise, all my skating skills and know-how immediately returned to me. Within minutes I was doing spins, skating backward, skating on one foot. I figured if I could master these stunts so easily, just imagine what I could do if I let go of the rail!

Giving myself one good push, I started out by faith. I was doing remarkably well, too, until the guy in front of me asked me to let go of his shirt.

Now with nothing to hold onto, I had only one choice.

"Push me," I said, jumping in front of a speed skater. He had a puzzled look on his face but obligingly gave me one quick shove that sent me flying. One lap, two laps, three laps. There was no stopping me now!

I was on my fourth lap when the "clear the floor" announcement came. I wasn't sure how to apply the brakes, but I knew it had something to do with the toes. Heading off the floor at Mach speed, I tried to lift my heels off the ground and stand on my toes. It worked. Sort of. It set me sailing through the air into a perfect double somersault over the snack bar counter. I could have just smiled and pretended I had done the flip on purpose, but since I landed on top of the Orange Whiz, I decided to just climb down and disappear into the crowd.

As I walked away, my legs began to cramp, my ankles began to swell, and my pride began to plummet. All I could think of was getting those skates off as fast as I could. Sure, we were only 10 minutes into the skate session, but at the rate I was going, "Hokey Pokey" would be suicide.

chapter twenty

the great **cover-up**

Of all summer activities, shopping for a new swimsuit is my least favorite. That's because I almost always get a saleslady with a sick sense of humor. The one I had last week was a prime example. I asked if she could suggest something that would make my body look good on the beach this summer. She said, "Sure. Bury most of it in the sand."

The clerk who waited on me yesterday was a little kinder. At least she *attempted* to compliment the suit I was trying on.

"You know," she said, "the way that material fan-folds at your waist is really quite stunning."

I would have thanked her, but unfortunately, it wasn't the material that was fan-folding. It was my waist.

Another problem with shopping for swim wear is the current fashion trend. Swimsuits have gotten smaller and smaller, so finding a modest one can be a real challenge—especially when you have a clerk like the one I had this morning.

"How about this little one?" she suggested, handing me what appeared to be an empty hanger.

"Where *is* it?" I asked, straining my eyes to see something.

"It's there . . . behind the price tag."

I looked and looked. Finally, I spotted it. It was one of those new string bathing suits.

"If I had wanted dental floss," I said as I handed it back to her, "I would have gone to the drugstore."

"Well, how 'bout *this* one?" she asked, holding up a tiny hot-pink number.

"That's a bathing suit?" I said in disbelief. "If I buy that, what will Barbie wear this summer?"

"Exactly what is it that you're looking for in a swimsuit?" she pressed, her patience wearing thinner by the moment.

"For one thing, some material," I pleaded.

"This new stretch swimsuit would be perfect for you then," she coaxed.

I tried it on but handed it back to her.

"You didn't like it either?" she sighed.

"Oh, it's pretty," I said. "But I wanted a swimsuit, not a tourniquet." Then I added, "What I'd *really* like is just a regular swimsuit. Don't you sell any of those anymore?"

She thought for a moment. "I think I may have the exact one you're looking for," she said, then walked to a nearby rack and picked out a sky-blue swimsuit with white trim. "How's this?" I couldn't believe it. It was perfect. Stylish, yet tasteful. Eye-catching, yet modest. It was my size, too, and even less expensive than the swimsuits with half the material.

"I'll take it," I announced happily.

"You know," she commented, as she totaled my purchase, "we've been selling a lot of this style lately. I wonder what's going on."

I handed her the money and smiled. "Maybe everyone's realizing that the ideal swimsuit is like ketchup to my cooking. The more it covers, the better it looks."

chapter twenty-one

are you sure **shakespeare** started like this?

To this day I don't understand why I didn't get a better grade in my ninth-grade English class. When our assignment was to write a poem, I wrote one:

> The food at my school's not so great;
> It really is quite second-rate.
> I ordered the fries

And to my surprise
They got up and crawled off my plate.

I wrote notable essays on such topics as "Erasing and How It Improved My Grades" and "Napping Your Way to Physical Fitness." These didn't impress my teacher, either.

When we were told to turn in three book reports during the semester, I turned them in. I didn't receive any credit for them, though, which I thought was unfair. After all, our teacher never told us we couldn't write about the yellow pages, the Sears catalog, and the TV Guide.

I should've received high marks during our study of classic literature. I knew about *Gone with the Wind.* It was the excuse I usually gave for missing homework assignments. I was familiar with *Romeo and Juliet.* (Weren't they those two new kids on campus?) I was acquainted with *Moby Dick,* too. I even ordered him a couple of times at Denny's.

I was an expert on grammar as well. But then, why shouldn't I be? Grammar and Grandper had been a part of my life for as long as I could remember.

I also knew the difference between "dessert" and "desert." A school cafeteria dessert will always have more sand than a desert.

"Dangling participles" was something I knew about. I seemed to get them whenever my hems weren't stitched properly.

I knew my vowels and how much Vanna White charges to buy one.

It was a cinch for me to find "misplaced modifiers." What I *couldn't* find were misplaced locker keys, misplaced lunch money, and misplaced gym shorts.

I knew about run-on sentences and how they seem to go on and on and on forever and ever without really saying anything new or interesting and how these only serve to exhaust the reader and should be edited out of all writing if the writer's work is to be taken seriously and if the writer wishes to receive a passing grade in the class where they are teaching how not to write run-on sentences. I knew all that. I—also knew, how important: punctuation, is; in "any" and all! writing? and how speling iz equalee emportent.

I was never too shy to share my writing with the entire class. Unfortunately, I did most of my sharing on the chalkboard and had to write whatever my teacher dictated. It was usually really creative—"I will not chew gum in class," and "I will never try to erase a freckle off the neck of the boy seated in front of me again."

I suppose the real reason I didn't get a good grade in that class had more to do with the annual spelling bee than anything else. I was disqualified on the very first word. But I filed a protest. The rules didn't say anything about having to spell our name.

chapter twenty-two

you are what you **munch**

Have you ever had a "munchie attack"? You know . . . that irresistible desire to eat an entire bag of potato chips all by yourself, then lick the inside of the bag? Have you ever snacked on so many dill pickles your lips had to be surgically unpuckered? Or downed enough Ding Dongs to chocolate-coat your tonsils?

If your answer is "yes," then you'll understand what I went

through the other night.

It was late. My family was asleep. The Doritos commercial had just aired on television, followed by the Keebler elves and that sweet-talker Betty Crocker. My defenses were down. I was vulnerable. That's when the attack hit.

I searched the cupboards and refrigerator for anything that met the "munchie criteria"—frosted, French-fried, or double-stuffed. Unfortunately, not a single munchable item was to be found. Oh, there were a few things in the vegetable drawer, but they weren't quite what I had in mind.

Don't get me wrong. I think carrots are wonderful. If held upright, they can conveniently carry four to five glazed donuts. Celery sticks are good, too. When all the spoons in the house are dirty, they're great for stirring Cool Whip. (The strings from a stalk of celery can also be pulled off and used as dental floss.)

Cucumbers are good for rolling out pie crusts. Asparagus stalks are handy for scooping the filling out of an éclair. And broccoli? Well, maybe George Bush was right about broccoli.

Anyway, the value and nutritional benefits of vegetables are not the issue here. I readily admit vegetables are healthy. It's just that on this particular night, I needed something more, well, you know, . . . more calorie-filled.

There was no time to lose. If left untreated, a munchie attack can led to more serious disorders, such as "Twinkie-nemia" or "S.O.D." (Severe Oreo Deficiency). So, I did what I had to do. I went "munchie shopping."

I hit the grocery store cookie aisle first. Three boxes of Fig Newtons, four packages of Chips Ahoy, and six bags of animal cookies later, it was on to the Dolly Madison display.

Then, the candy bin, and lastly, the ice cream aisle. I grabbed Klondike bars, ice cream sandwiches, push-up yogurt, and every other ice cream novelty I could find.

By now, my cart looked like a Good Humor truck, so I started toward the checkout stand. On my way, I grabbed several bags of potato chips and some butterscotch pudding for dip. Now, I figured I had just enough goodies to put the munchies into remission.

As the clerk ran each item over the scanner, she couldn't help but inquire, "Having a party?"

"No," I confessed. "I just needed a few things."

Then she asked the inevitable question. "Do you want plastic or paper bags?"

I thought for a moment.

"Neither," I smiled. "I'll be eating it here."

chapter twenty-three

off the road **again**

Like most teens, I couldn't wait to get my driver's license. My first step toward this goal was to pass Driver's Education and Driver's Training. For me, this was no easy trick.

You see, I'm not what you'd call a natural-born driver. Oh, I can stop on a dime, but it's usually in some pedestrian's pocket. I'm only kidding. I watch out for pedestrians. I just wish they wouldn't hog so much of the sidewalk.

My high school driving instructor did his best to teach me the laws of the road and the proper way to operate a vehicle. It wasn't his fault I was such a bad driver. (I managed to get four tickets my first day behind the wheel—and that was on the simulator!)

The classes weren't totally wasted, though. I did pick up a few bits of driving knowledge. For instance, in Driver's Education, I learned a good driver pictures the steering wheel as the face of her watch, then places her hands at the ten o'clock and two o'clock positions. (Looking back, this could have been my problem. I had a digital watch.)

I learned a broken yellow line means it's all right to pass. It doesn't mean the street painter had hiccups.

I also learned that whenever an ambulance is behind me, I should pull over to the right and stop—not flag the driver down and give him directions to the school cafeteria.

In my Driver's Training class I learned, the hard way, never to exit a vehicle without first shifting into the park gear and engaging the emergency brake. I failed to do this once and my car went for a spin without me. I wouldn't have minded so much, but it ended up getting a better grade for the day than I did!

Driver's Training also showed me how unimaginative our town was. Every single street I turned onto was either named "Wrong Way" or "Do Not Enter."

Somehow, though, I managed to pass both classes. (Frankly, I think my Driver's Training instructor passed me just so he wouldn't have to endure me for another semester.)

I even went on to pass the official state driving test. I won't tell you how many tries it took, but let's just say I spent so much time at the Department of Motor Vehicles they issued me my own parking space.

When I finally earned my driver's license, I couldn't help but feel proud. So proud I promised myself I would never take it for granted. I'd show my appreciation by being a cautious driver, a defensive driver, a safe driver. Over the years I believe I've become just that. As a matter of fact, I even say a prayer every time I drive the freeways. My family appreciates this. They just wish I'd open my eyes a little more often while I'm doing it.

chapter twenty-four

when you're **hot**, you're hot

Unless you live in the Arctic, each of us will endure at least one heat wave sometime during our life. So you won't be caught off guard, you'll know you're in a heat wave when:

- You smile and your braces melt.
- Your Jacuzzi is bubbling at 112 degrees and you haven't even turned it on yet.

- You stare into your freezer for hours on end.
- You suddenly get an uncontrollable desire to ride a ceiling fan.
- You start using block ice for a pillow.
- You get a tan just watching the weather report on television.
- Your parakeet starts wearing a visor and Ray-Bans.
- Your dog still chases the neighborhood cats, only now he wants you to pull him in a wagon while he does it.
- You sit down in your car and permanently brand the design of the upholstery into the back of your thighs.
- You get in line at car washes . . . even without a car.
- Your frozen dinner cooks itself on your way home from the store.
- You spend most of the day in an air-conditioned mall. That is, until the security guard complains that your lounge chair is blocking the aisle.
- You can hear your feet sizzle when you walk barefoot down the street.
- Your lips have more cracks than the San Andreas Fault.
- You've bought enough iced tea to reenact the Boston Tea Party.
- Your favorite place to spend the evening is on top of your lawn sprinklers.
- The most strenuous exercise you feel like doing is hand-to-mouth Popsicle lifts.
- You need an oven mitten to open your car door.
- Your body temperature sets off the smoke alarm in your house.
- You've replaced the shoulder pads in all your dresses and

shirts with ice packs.

- But you *really* know you're in a heat wave when you don't even mind that giant pimple that just popped up on your forehead. You're for *anything* that'll give you a little shade.

chapter twenty-five
oral reports
(and other near-death experiences)

My number-one fear in school was oral reports. (The cafeteria fish sticks ran a close second.)

Standing in front of my class for five minutes sharing everything I know about a given subject wasn't easy for me. For one thing, I could never figure out how to fill the remaining four minutes and thirty-nine seconds.

My most memorable oral report happened in the ninth grade.

To say I was nervous that day would be a gross understatement. I was sweating so much I almost drowned everyone in the front row.

But I had reason to be nervous. Just before I began my oral report, my teacher informed the class that "ums" and "uhs" wouldn't count toward our 1,000-word requirement. This may not have affected the other students, but there went half of my speech.

As if that wasn't bad enough, I also had to contend with the cut-up in the back of the class. You know who I mean. Every class has one—the guy who makes goofy faces and disruptive noises with his armpits throughout everyone's speech. I would have told my teacher on him, but he *was* my teacher.

My voice was another problem. Whenever I get extremely nervous, my voice tends to go up an octave. Or to put it in more descriptive terms, I start out sounding like Barbara Walters and end up like Alvin the Chipmunk.

Thanks to all my oral report mishaps, though, I've prepared the following list of tips, which I am now ready to pass on.

The Cafeteria Lady's Tips for Terrific Oral Reports

- Speak clearly. (Mumbling won't get you anything in life . . . except maybe a job repeating orders into the microphone at drive-through restaurants.)
- Don't be afraid to move around during your speech. (Leaving the room, however, might result in a lower grade.)
- Never repeat yourself.
- Never repeat yourself. (Did I already say that?)
- Use 3x5-inch cards. (Not only do they help a speaker stay

on track, but they're also great for fanning her back to consciousness should she pass out from stage fright.)

- If you're one of the super-nervous, consider presenting your speech in the form of a rap. (Then when your knees start knocking and your heart begins to pound, the class will think it's just part of the beat.)
- Look at the audience. (This makes them feel included, as well as assuring you that they're still present.)
- Timing is of the utmost importance. (Should the audience start throwing tomatoes, you need to know precisely when to duck.)
- Share a few anecdotes. (Be careful not to confuse an anecdote with an antidote. An anecdote is a funny story that illustrates your point. An antidote is what follows one of my meals.)
- Never speak beyond your allotted time. (Remember this is an oral report, not a telephone conversation!)

chapter twenty-six

one **cool** turkey

I remember the first year my mother let me cook our Thanksgiving turkey all by myself. It was my reward for not having caused a single fire in Foods class all week. (True, we were doing salads that week and it's hard to set a gelatin mold ablaze, but that's beside the point.)

This was my chance to prove to our family once and for all that "Toxic Waste on Toast" wasn't the only dish I could prepare. It

97

was my opportunity to show them that whatever goes into my oven doesn't necessarily have to explode. It was my moment to triumph in the kitchen and not have it involve emergency room service.

Dad believed in me. "I know you can do it, kid," he said while dialing Pizza Man to put him on standby. My sisters were equally trusting. "But, Mom," they whined, "we still have chipped teeth from that time we sampled her pudding." My big brother was the only one who actually believed I could do it. Why else would he spend the entire morning telling me to "stuff it"?

Whatever the reason for their doubts, I was determined to prove them wrong. I was going to make them eat crow, uh, I mean turkey.

The recipe indicated the first step was to wash the turkey. Simple enough, although I *did* have a hard time fitting it in the dishwasher.

The next step was to remove the bag of gizzards, liver and other parts from the bird. (Why they can't put a toy surprise in there instead is beyond me.) I reached my hand in as far as I could but couldn't find the bag. Figuring it must have gotten washed away during the rinse cycle, I moved on to step number three—dressing the turkey.

The recipe didn't specify casual or formal, so I chose a simple bow tie. (The vest and knee pants kept falling off him anyway.)

Now it was time to "baste" the turkey. Not knowing what "baste" meant, I consulted a dictionary. In there, I discovered the word basically means to "butter something up." So, I started.

"Hey, big guy, you're quite a looker." "What great wings!

You must be a weight lifter." "Are there are more like you at home?"

I had to stop right there. Any more buttering up and the bird would have asked for my home phone number. And believe me, I already had enough turkeys calling me.

The final step was to place him in a preheated oven and leave him there for five hours. Exactly five hours later, I called my family in for the big moment.

"Docsn't hc look cool?" I bragged, removing him from the oven and adjusting his bow tie.

"*Too* cool," my mother said, feeling a drumstick. "He's still frozen."

"That's impossible!" I insisted. "He's been in there for five hours."

"Cooking at 350 degrees?" my mother asked.

"Of course not," I explained confidently. "The recipe just said to preheat the oven. It didn't say anything about leaving it on."

Luckily, Pizza Man was already en route.

slumber party **etiquette**

Ever wonder what the proper behavior is for slumber parties? What you should do? What you shouldn't do?

Here are my official etiquette tips for sleepovers:

- Sneaking six cans of Silly String into the party is considered improper behavior. Everyone knows it takes at least *12* cans to really have fun.

- Rolling up your best friend's sleeping bag is a polite thing to do, but make sure you say "Excuse me" if she's still in it at the time.
- It's always fun to give manicures and style wild hairdos at slumber parties. But if the cat won't sit still, then just do it to each other.
- When ordering pizzas, remember M & Ms don't go that well with pepperoni. They taste much better with anchovies and sauerkraut.
- Pillow fights should always be evenly matched. In other words, never more than eight girls to a chaperon.
- Whispering all night about that cute new guy in your youth group is considered rude and selfish behavior. After all, if you talk too softly, how can the adults in the house eavesdrop?
- Rubber spiders should never be placed on the pillows of fellow party-goers. They're much more effective dangling from the ceiling.
- If one of the attendees snores, rolling her over could solve the problem. However, recording her and playing it back the next morning over breakfast is much more entertaining.
- Tickling the feet of friends while they're asleep can be hazardous to your health—especially if their odor-eaters expired three months ago.
- Under no circumstances whatsoever should you give a single "wet willie" to those who've fallen asleep before you. They have two ears; give them two.
- The noise level should be kept to a minimum. If the fire department complains that they can't hear their sirens over the laughter coming from your party, maybe it's

time to tone it down a decibel or two.

• And finally, anyone who willfully consumes eight hot dogs, three bags of potato chips, twelve Cokes, and fourteen brownies during the night will be solely responsible for the expense of widening the front door so she can leave in the morning.

chapter twenty-eight

to brown-bag or **not** to brown-bag

I'm sure school cafeteria food has improved over the years, but in my day, school lunches left a lot to be desired. They were so bad that whenever we'd shoo a fly away, he'd thank us for it. In fact, I once watched a troop of ants form the words "Eat at Your Own Risk" as they marched by the cafeteria doors. No wonder our principal offered a discount on school insurance to any student who brown-bagged it.

To this day, I can still remember the cafeteria menu. Monday was burrito day. We had great burritos. Not to eat, mind you, but to stick under the legs of uneven lunch benches.

On Tuesdays we were served chicken and dumplings. Of course, if the P.E. Department ever ran low on baseballs, we had to make do without the dumplings.

Wednesday was the day for American ravioli. This dish wasn't too bad, although I didn't care for the way it made my tray sag.

On Thursday I always had squash for lunch. Not the regular kind of squash. That was just how my cheeseburger ended up when the guys got through playing "keep away" with it.

And finally, Friday was fish day. Now, I'm not accusing them of serving old fish sticks, but I once found a note from Jonah in one of them.

Some days, they'd try sneaking in a substitute food item like "Garden Surprise." (They named it that because they were surprised when anyone ordered it.) Another frequent substitute was macaroni and cheese. But I don't think they used real cheese. I'm not sure what they used, but I seem to recall a similar-looking substance in science class. We used it to clean the rust off lab tools.

If we didn't like the main course, we could order à la carte items like pizza. My school had the toughest pizza crust you can imagine. I won't go into detail, but let's just say we had a good idea where all our old textbooks ended up.

Grilled cheese sandwiches were another à la yuck item. After one bite, we'd end up throwing it to the birds. They, of course, would throw it back.

At most schools nowadays, students get to choose from

milk, chocolate milk, all kinds of sodas, New York seltzers, and more. At my school, we had only milk. And there was no freshness dating back then. We just figured the milk wasn't any good when we had to hammer the straw into it.

School officials knew how bad the food was. The school nurse sent more students home from C.F.S. (Cafeteria Food Syndrome) than from any other ailment. One student even broke his foot in the school cafeteria. He dropped a muffin on it.

Still, there was one good thing about our cafeteria food. It really boosted the school's student store profits. They made a fortune off the Pepto-Bismol sales!

chapter twenty-nine

making a **joyful** noise

In high school, I took one semester of band. I would have signed up for another semester, but the city passed an ordinance against it.

Don't think for a second that my music wasn't appreciated—it was. Thanks to my daily trumpet practices, no one seemed to mind the airport noise anymore. But it wasn't my fault I kept hitting the wrong note. Someone had killed a fly on my sheet music, and it looked exactly like a B-flat.

The trumpet wasn't the only wind instrument I played. My teacher tried me out on all of them. He said playing a wind instrument would be the perfect way to put all my hot air to good use. He also knew I could hold my breath for long periods of time. (Obviously, he'd seen me carrying my gym clothes home every Friday.)

One day, though, I caught the neighborhood dogs trying to bury my trumpet, so I figured it was time to switch to the trombone. I was doing pretty well on it, too, until the girl in front of me complained that I was rearranging the part in her hair every time I extended the slide.

The tuba was next, but I had to give that up as well. No matter how hard I tried, I could never get it to fit in my backpack.

The tuba was followed by the clarinet, the oboe, the bassoon, and the saxophone. Somehow, I managed to get good enough on the sax to play in one of the local parades. Unfortunately, though, they put me in the first row of the band directly behind the show horses. I won't say how I did, but I understand that to this day some townsfolk still talk about the stampede.

I quickly moved on to the English horn, the piccolo, and the flute. The flute wasn't bad. I discovered I could even play by ear. It's true. Every time I brought it up to my mouth, I'd accidentally stick it in the ear of the kid marching next to me.

Clearly, wind instruments weren't for me, so my teacher decided to try me out in the percussion section. I immediately requested the cymbals, figuring if I couldn't master *that* skill, I could still use them as giant Frisbees. The cymbals didn't work out, either. It seemed I was always crashing them together at the wrong moment—you know, like during English class.

Drums were my last chance. I practiced and practiced and practiced. All that effort paid off, too, because it wasn't long before I was allowed to march and play during half-time at one of our football games. Everyone was excited for me. As a matter of fact, it was the first time the entire football team ever carried a *band member* off the field. Naturally, I was flattered. But I still say they should have waited until after the song was over.

chapter thirty

the annual **VOW** exchange

Turning over new leaves isn't something I do only on January 1st. I turn them over all year long . . . every time I sweep the floor in my bedroom!

Those kinds of leaves are easy to turn over. The other kind—the resolutions, vows, and promises I make to myself each New Year—are much harder.

Most of my resolutions go through a series of rewrites

throughout the year. I start out with the best of intentions in January, but something happens as the months roll by, and I end up altering the majority of my vows. The process goes something like this:

January 1:	I vow to do 100 sit-ups every day.
June 1:	I vow to do 50 sit-ups every day.
December 1:	I vow to sit up sometime during the day.

January 1:	I will keep my room spotless all year.
June 1:	I will keep my room livable all year.
December 1:	Is that a bowling ball under my bed or a giant dustball?

January 1:	I'm going to rid myself of 10 unwanted pounds.
June 1:	I'm going to rid myself of five unwanted pounds.
December 1:	I'm going to rid myself of my bathroom scale.

January 1:	I will not sleep in past 8 A.M.
June 1:	I will not sleep in past noon.
December 1 :	I will not . . . zzz.

January 1:	I'm going to cook meals that taste better than the food at a gourmet restaurant.
June 1:	I'm going to cook meals that taste better than the food at the school cafeteria.
December 1:	I'm going to cook meals that taste better than the plate.

January 1:	I will not talk longer than two hours on the

	telephone every night.
June 1:	I will not talk longer than three hours on the telephone every night.
December 1:	I can't cut back on my phone calls. AT&T would never survive the revenue loss.

January 1:	I will eat two of each of the four food groups at every meal.
June 1:	I will eat one of each of the four food groups at every meal.
December 1:	I will find a way to chocolate-coat all items from the four food groups.

January 1:	I'm going to clean out my closet so everything will be in its proper place.
June 1:	I'm going to clean out my closet so the moths will have elbow room.
December 1:	I'm going to clean out my closet so I can find my husband.

January 1:	I vow to do aerobics for 30 minutes each day.
June 1:	I vow to do aerobics for 15 minutes each day.
December 1:	I vow to watch an aerobics video . . . through the opening credits at least.

January 1:	I vow to brush and floss my teeth after every meal.
June 1:	I vow to brush my teeth once a day.
December 1:	Didn't I used to have teeth?

January 1:	I vow to finish every single thing that I start.
June 1:	I vow to finish most of the things that I start.
December 1:	I vow to . . . (I'll get back to this later).

chapter thirty-one

how's the **weather** up there?

It was obvious from birth that I was going to be tall. The doctor had to put an extension on my incubator, and the footprints on my birth certificate said, "Continued next page."

What surprised people, though, was how quickly I grew. I outgrew my car seat on my way home from the hospital and my crib by the time I was a month old. My first step crossed two ZIP codes, and whenever I sat in my high chair, my feet dragged on the floor. My growth chart didn't even fit in our house. Mom had to hang it on the side of a high rise.

Don't get me wrong. There are a lot of positives about being tall. You're easy to spot in a crowd, you never have to worry about someone in front of you blocking your view, and in some sports, height can really give you an edge.

Being tall gave me an edge in the long jump. I could jump farther than any of my classmates. That mile-and-a-half walk back to school after I landed was always a drag, though.

I was the best swimmer in school, too. I could do a lap with just one butterfly stroke. I might even have made the team, but the coach said I confused the other swimmers every time I referred to the eight-foot-deep section as the "shallow end."

I *did* make it on the basketball team. I was pretty good, too, scoring more points than all the other players combined. But I eventually had to quit. My doctor said all that stooping down to make the baskets was giving me back problems.

The fact that I was tall and thin got me a spot on the pole-vaulting team. Sure, it was just as the pole, but all athletes have to start somewhere.

Being my height does have a few drawbacks. Ducking 747s is just one of them. Finding clothes that fit is another one. I have a lot in common with Noah—I usually dress like I'm expecting a flood, too. It is nearly impossible to find pants that are long enough for me. No matter how hard I try, they only hit about mid calf. I realize *some* pants look good like that, but they didn't when I was younger—bell-bottoms were in!

Another disadvantage of being tall is having to put up with all sorts of rude comments—stuff like "What'd you do? Rise to the occasion and forget to come back down?" or "How's the weather up there?"

That last one is the most common and most irritating. But whenever someone asks me that, I don't let it bother me. I simply smile and answer, "It must be snowing, 'cause I just heard from a flake."

chapter thirty-two

red, white, and **picnic** blues

One of the best ways to celebrate our nation's freedom is with a good old-fashioned Fourth of July picnic. There's nothing quite like dining outdoors with family, friends, and enough ants to carry off a Winnebago. I realize ants and picnics tend to go together. I just don't enjoy arm wrestling one over a celery stick.

But even with the ants and the elements, Fourth of July picnics are a lot of fun . . . especially if you play all the traditional picnic games.

The first game you should play is the water balloon toss. This is an easy way to make sure everyone washes his hands before dinner.

Follow that with the wheelbarrow race. This is where you walk on your hands while a friend carries your feet. Not only is this a good picnic game, it's also a great way to keep your new Reeboks from getting grass stains on them.

Potato sack races are fun, too, even though I seldom win. (Okay, maybe I should remove the contents first, but can you think of an easier way to mash potatoes?)

Another popular game is tug-of-war. My sister and I used to love playing this. But not just at picnics. We played it every time we wanted to wear the same outfit.

The game I'm most skilled at is the egg toss. That's to be expected, though. With my cooking, I've had a lot of experience with people throwing food at me.

Speaking of food, what would a Fourth of July picnic be without the traditional potluck dinner? Potlucks are great because people bring their favorite foods, then everyone shares. My family has no trouble spotting my dish. They just look for the one the flies are picketing.

Once the games are over, the food has been eaten, and the sun has set, it's time for the highlight of the day—the annual fireworks display!

Most city parks put on quite a spectacular fireworks show. Ours even had a parachutist last year. I'll never forget it. He landed right on top of our picnic table. The poor guy broke his foot in three places.

The sad part is he might have escaped without any injury whatsoever, but unfortunately, he landed on one of my cupcakes.

chapter thirty-three

love——the long and short of it

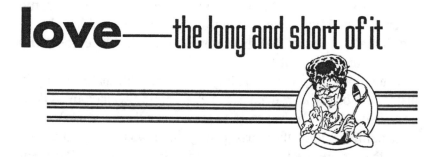

When I was in school, cute guys were always flipping for me. They said it was part of their gymnastics routine, but I knew better.

Okay, if you want to know the truth, I mostly attracted geeks—you know, the type of guy who has bleu cheese dressing running down the side of his mouth . . . when he's not even eating.

I remember the very first boy who ever asked me out. He

put the eek! in geek. His one talent in life was being able to play "On Top of Old Smoky" by squeezing his hand under his armpit. Now, granted that skill may look impressive on a job application, but enduring two solid hours of it doesn't make for a fun date. I think he had some sort of skin condition, too. Every time I told him to flake off, he did.

Being tall for my age presented another problem—most of the boys in my grade were shorter than me. One guy who asked me to a school Valentine's Day party was so short I figured I'd have to spend the entire evening giving him a boost up to the punch bowl. So I turned him down. I wanted to be available for that cute boy in my English class, anyway. Surely, he would ask me to the party. After all, wasn't he always passing me notes that said how he could get lost in our love? (All right, he didn't really write all that. He shortened it to just "Get lost," but I knew what he meant.)

If he didn't ask me to the party, there was still that new boy in math—the one who winked at me every time I walked by. (Okay, he actually closed *both* eyes, but I took it as a double wink.)

If neither one of them asked me, there was always that guy with the gorgeous blue eyes in my Spanish class. He sent romantic notes to me every day, too. ("Adios, salsa-face" does mean "I love you" in Spanish, doesn't it?)

To my surprise, not one of those boys asked me to the Valentine's party. I ended up agreeing to go with the boy half my size. And you know what? He turned out to be a really nice guy. He even brought me a corsage. (He had to pole-vault his way up to my shoulder to pin it on, but it was still a thoughtful gesture.)

Once at the party, it soon became obvious that I had the best date of all. That cute guy in my English class decided to pick a fight with his date, and they both had a lousy time. That new boy in my math class made a pig out of himself at the refreshment table and ate everything in sight . . . including the cardboard centerpiece. And ol' Blue Eyes from my Spanish class stood up his date completely.

That night I discovered something very important. It doesn't matter if someone's short or tall, good-looking or not. All that matters is what kind of a person he is inside.

Yes, despite the difference in our heights, I had a terrific time with my date that night. We talked, we laughed, we even ended up seeing eye-to-eye on a lot of issues. Well, at least eye-to-kneecap.

chapter thirty-four

'tis the **season** to burn fruitcakes

The holiday season means plenty of homemade pies, fruitcakes, and eggnog. Around our house, it also means plenty of Pepto-Bismol, Rolaids, and Tums.

Holiday cooking is not one of my talents. My Christmas tree cookies taste like lumber and leave tiny splinters in your tongue. My gingerbread houses could make a termite gag. And not even Abraham Lincoln could saw through one of my chocolate Yule logs.

My eggnog turns out awful, too. But I think I've finally figured out what I've been doing wrong. This year, I'm not going to scramble the eggs first.

The biggest problem I have with holiday foods is overcooking. I don't roast chestnuts over an open fire. I cremate them. In fact, I've burned so many Yuletide goodies it's no wonder my smoke alarm plays "It's Beginning to Look a Lot Like Christmas."

I get plenty of requests for my fruitcakes, though. With that hole in the middle, people say they're a perfect addition to their weight sets.

For years I've been sending these homemade delicacies, edible or not, to my friends and relatives as gifts. But last Christmas, the post office ordered me to stop. They said lifting boxes of my pumpkin bread was resulting in far too many employee back injuries.

My holiday cooking disasters aren't a total loss, though, for they inspired the following poem. (You may want to have a tissue handy as you read it.)

> 'Twas the night before Christmas,
> And all through the house
> Roared the flames from my kitchen—
> Too many to douse.
>
> My oven exploded;
> I started to run.
> Then realized that just meant
> My cookies were done.

My hot apple turnovers
Also looked grim,
After seven whole hours
Of flame-broiling them.

My mince pie looked great,
An out-and-out hit.
But it took a chain saw
To cut into it.

And I thought my nut bread
Had reached a new high,
Till flies took a whiff
And dropped out of the sky.

My gelatin mold
Never seemed to get done.
And my homemade pound cake.
Weighed more like a ton.

And what did my cranberry
Coffee cake lack
That so many ants
Would bring the crumbs back?

So maybe I'll hang up
My apron this year . . .
And let all my friends
Have a "healthy" new year!

chapter thirty-five

I flip for **fashion** shows

When I was 15, my mom decided I should attend a charm and modeling school so I could learn to walk with grace, poise, and dignity . . . or at least without getting my legs tangled up. Mom thought the eight-week course would be good for me. I'd learn fashion trends, makeup tips, and perhaps even develop a little class. So with high hopes for a new me in just two months' time, Mom enrolled me in the course. "You'll graduate with flying colors," she assured me.

The school turned out to be easier than I imagined. That's because I already knew most of what they taught.

They gave us simple fashion pointers, such as telling us running shoes should never be worn with an evening gown. (I knew that. Bowling shoes are much more attractive with formal attire.)

They taught us that having a run in your nylons is a definite fashion no-no. (I already knew that, too. Although, if you make six or seven more runs, you can pretend they're a design.)

They even taught us table manners, such as which fork you should use for your salad. (This answer was easy—your own, of course!)

And they gave us tips on makeup application. (My tip was to use a mop.)

The eight weeks passed rather quickly, and before I knew it, it was graduation night and time for the big fashion show for our parents and guests. Each student would model fashions provided by a local boutique. I was scheduled to be last on the program, modeling a stunning floor-length beaded gown.

Backstage, I tried to remain calm. This was just a fashion show. What's the worst that could happen?

Finally, the instructor called my name. I held my head high and stepped out from behind the curtain. Smiling to the audience, I made my way down the runway. I turned where I should turn. I pivoted where I should pivot. Every movement was graceful and fluid. I could hear the "oohs" and "aahs" coming from the audience.

Then . . . it happened. My right foot slipped, taking my left foot with it. I ended up doing a double somersault with a half-twist, landing on the lap of a man in the front row.

I felt embarrassed. But mostly, I felt sorry for my mother who had wanted me to graduate with flying colors, not graduate flying. But Mom was very understanding. She said I had given it my all. I had put my best food forward. Could I help it if it kept on going? Besides, she said I should take comfort in the fact that only local newspaper reporters were present.

She also pointed out that it was evident I had learned something in charm school, after all. She said I managed to retain excellent posture throughout the entire incident.

chapter thirty-six

when life gets a **bit** testy

I never looked forward to finals—you know, those tests that help teachers determine whether you've picked up anything from their class besides the flu and two eye infections.

Science finals were the most difficult for me—not that I didn't spend plenty of time in my science book. I did. Opened to page 256, it made a great pillow.

For some reason, though, I could never remember your most

basic scientific facts—like the order of the planets. I knew Pluto was out there somewhere. I just wasn't sure if it came before or after Goofy and Grumpy.

Health class finals were also challenging. When asked what a "balanced meal" was, I said it meant having a Big Mac in one hand and a chocolate shake of the same weight in the other.

What made math finals so hard were all those word problems. I recall one in particular. "If there are 30 students in your class and each one gives you two dollars, what would you have?" I answered "FUN!" The teacher marked it wrong. Go figure.

Our final for physical education was to run two laps around the field. I didn't fare too well on this test, either. All the other students finished in 12 minutes or less. I finished the following semester.

I'm proud to say I typed 55 words per minute on my typing class final. That *would* have been an "A" if only my fingers had been on the right keys.

My Foods class final was probably the easiest. It had simple questions like "Name the three most important utensils in a kitchen." For me, that was the fire extinguisher, a stomach pump, and a telephone with an automatic dial set to 9-1-1. (My teacher was aware of my cooking talents and counted this correct.)

One thing I learned about finals is that studying for them while watching TV isn't a good idea. I discovered this the hard way. On one of my history finals I inadvertently listed Gilligan as our 14th president and Mr. Ed as the first Speaker of the House. Not only did I receive a poor grade, but I was also sent to the counselor's office for evaluation.

Another tip I can pass along is to get plenty of sleep before your final. I should point out, however, that this isn't a good idea while the teacher is handing out the exams.

They say eating a good breakfast before taking your test also helps. I'm sure this is true, but the year I tried it, my teacher just took the waffle iron off my desk and told me to get to work.

However you prepare for your finals, the important thing is to do your best. I *tried* doing my best, but that special incentive program my school offered always hindered me. It was their policy that all students receiving a "B" or better on their finals would be awarded free cafeteria lunches for a week.

No wonder we all wanted a "C."

chapter thirty-seven

a **star** is hatched

I remember the first Thanksgiving play I was cast in. The director was so smitten by my exceptional acting talent that he awarded me what he termed "the most important part in the play."

The most important part in the play! I thought to myself. *This is great! Why, I'll be spending so much time in the spotlight, I'll get a tan! I'll be signing so many autographs, my fingers will get cramps!*

"The turkey?" I said in disbelief as the director handed me the script. "You want me to play the *turkey?*"

"You'll be perfect for the role," he assured me, glancing down at my legs. "Rehearsals begin next Friday at three o'clock sharp. Be there!"

Now I didn't want to get my feathers ruffled over this, but I couldn't understand why he would waste my remarkable dramatic abilities on such a simple role. And what about all the ridicule I was sure to face? I could hear it now: the other actors telling me to "stuff it," or the director telling me my acting was for the "birds" and sending me to my "dressing" room.

Reading through the script only added insult to injury. My only speaking line was "Gobble, gobble." (Actually, it was just one gobble, but I protested so much the director finally agreed to expand the part.)

At each rehearsal, I tried to convince him to expand it even further—you know, add a song or two. Something like (to the tune of "Take Me Out to the Ball Game"):

"Take me out of the microwave.
Take me out 'cause I'm hot.
I was invited over for brunch,
But no one told me that I would be lunch!"

Or,

"Home, home on the range . . .
Till the Thanksgiving menu is changed."

I even volunteered to get the audience in an early Yuletide spirit by singing, "Drumsticks roasting on an open fire . . . "

But the director turned down all of my suggestions. He said I was supposed to be a turkey, not a ham. All he wanted me to do was walk on stage, say my line, then exit.

It was hardly a role to gain the attention of the Tony award committee, but I was stuck. My parents had already bought a movie camera, lights, and 14 rolls of film for the occasion. (Parents do this sort of thing so they'll have something to show at every social gathering you attend for the rest of your life!)

This particular home movie is one I wish had been lost over the years, but I wasn't that lucky. Not that the play itself was a flop. It wasn't. The set was very realistic, the costumes turned out great, and everyone recited their lines without a single miss. Everyone but me, that is. When it came time for me to speak, I couldn't remember my line. Was it "Gabble, gabble," "Goodle, goodle"? My mind went so blank, I would have had to look at the program even to remember my name.

After what seemed like an eternity, all the pilgrims turned their muskets toward me. I figured that was my cue to run off-stage. I didn't stop running, though, until I was safe at home.

I learned a lot about humility that day. I learned that no matter how small the part, each person and each line is important.

So, the next month when they held the Christmas pageant auditions and I was cast as the donkey, I didn't protest one bit. Besides, I figured "Eeehaw!" would be a lot easier to remember!

chapter thirty-eight

laps or **naps**

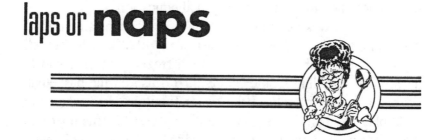

I hate to admit it, but P.E. wasn't my best subject in school. My heart pounded, I sweated profusely, and I ended up panting so loudly they could hear me all the way to the cafeteria. And that was just from trying to get my gym locker open.

You see, I wasn't exactly what you'd call physically fit. I took naps between sit-ups and thought the definition of "muscle tone" was the pitch my thighs hit when they slammed together during jumping jacks.

My least favorite of all P.E. activities was running laps. I was always the last one to finish. In fact, a few times my teacher didn't even wait for me to complete my final lap. She just handed the stopwatch to the school custodian and went home.

I wasn't only slow when it came to physical activity. I was accident-prone, too. My P.E. uniform was a neck brace and 12 yards of Ace bandages. My mother had to write so many notes requesting restricted activity for me that I started thinking P.E. stood for "Please Excuse."

But just because I was the only one in my class with a lifetime subscription to "Sports Injuries Illustrated," and just because I held the school record for the two-day mile, I still understood the importance of physical education.

The body I was building in junior high was the same body I was going to have to live in the rest of my life. So, I had to tell myself that a push-up was more than frozen yogurt. I had to decide that dribbling would be a skill I'd use on the basketball court, instead of merely at the water fountain. And whenever we'd play baseball, I was going to do my best to remember that those little white squares out on the field were bases, not pillows.

Yes, I had to realize that P.E. was necessary for good health and a good outlook on life. Besides, I knew if I didn't build up my strength, I'd never be able to lift the rolls in the school cafeteria!

chapter thirty-nine

oh, no! oh, no! it's off to **work** I go!

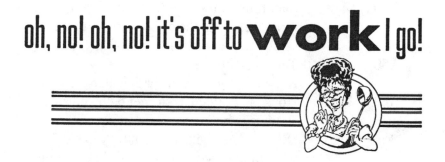

My very first job was to baby-sit three boys, ages eight, six, and five. These guys were such terrors they made Saddam Hussein look like Mister Rogers.

I accepted the job without knowing their last two baby-sitters had to undergo extensive therapy. One had developed a severe drool, and the other started talking to street lights. Their mother, though, assured me the boys were well-behaved and kept to a very strict schedule. Figuring a "strict schedule" meant dinner by 7 P.M. and bed by 9 P.M., I agreed to the job. Boy, did I make a mistake!

Oh, they were on a schedule all right, but it was more like:

7:04	Tie the baby-sitter to a chair and put a gag in her mouth.
7:05 to 7:30	Squirt her with Silly String and water pistols.
7:33	Order six pizzas from six different pizzerias. Eat four of them; play Frisbee with the other two.
8:10 to 9:45	Play four quarters of football in the living room, breaking the coffee table into the same number of quarters.
9:50	Turn on bath water.
10:30	Remember to turn off bath water.
10:33	House is flooded, so forget bath and surf straight to bed.
10:40 to 11:00	"Story time." This is when they decide what kind of story they're going to tell their parents as to why the house is such a mess.
11:05	"Lights out." They have no choice. The flooding from the bathtub caused all the lamps to short-circuit.

I never baby-sat for them again.

My next experience with the work force was at a fast-food restaurant. I worked the drive-through microphone first, but since I couldn't talk with a jawbreaker in my mouth and I got more than 10 percent of the orders right, they immediately moved me to the grill.

I didn't mind working the grill. I picked up a lot of good cooking tips there—tips I still use to this very day. Like putting barbecue sauce in the fire extinguisher. This brilliant technique not only puts the fire out but bastes the meat at the same time.

It was soon time to move on, though, and the next job I landed was secretarial. My application must have impressed the boss because he hired me on the spot. He noted, too, that my bilingual skills could be an asset to the company. It was a fun job until that inevitable day when he discovered I wasn't typing a foreign language at all. I was just hitting all the wrong keys on the typewriter!

Today, however, I can finally say I have the job of my dreams. All I do is write and sign autographs all day long. Of course, most of the writing I do is in my checkbook and all my autographs are on charge card slips, but at least no one's tying me to a chair and putting a gag in my mouth. (Okay, on several occasions my editors have tried, but so far I've been too fast for them!)

chapter forty

don't laugh ... I made it **myself**

Every Christmas, I enjoy making gifts for my family and friends. Unfortunately, no one enjoys receiving them.

Let's see. There were the sugar cookies in the shape of Christmas trees (and harder to bite through), the fudge that had to be chiseled out of its gift box, and the homemade jelly beans that ate a hole through everyone's Christmas stockings. Then, there were the items that didn't turn out so great.

151

I'll never forget the year I baked little zucchini bread loaves for everyone. My dad was the only one who appreciated them. He said they saved him a fortune on bricks for the new patio.

Another year, my mother really liked the gingerbread houses I made—the ones with those cute little chimneys. But, I had to tell her they didn't have chimneys. They were just still smoking from being left in the oven too long.

When the next Yuletide season rolled around, I thought I'd try my hand at knitting. I made sweaters for my entire family. Did they appreciate them? No. All they did was complain because I forgot a simple little thing like the hole for their heads to go through.

My sister wasn't impressed with the seashell necklace I made for her that year, either. All right, so maybe I should have removed the seaweed first . . .

I tried to make it up to her the following Christmas with a pair of biodegradable avocado pit earrings. She wasn't impressed. She didn't like the fact that every time she turned her head too quickly, she ended up with two black eyes. I tried to tell her that was a small price to pay for high fashion, but she still wasn't interested.

My uncle wasn't thrilled with the coffee mug I made for him one Christmas. And no wonder. It had so many leaks, he could drink from it and take his morning shower at the same time.

Grandmother hated the dress I made for her that year, too. She thought I should have hemmed it with a needle and thread, instead of all those paper clips.

This year, though, things are going to be different. Each and every gift I give is going to have a store label. You won't find me handing out any more home-baked goodies or one-of-a-kind earrings. You won't see me giving away items I've knitted, crocheted, or sewed. Unless, of course, I can get this shirt I'm making for my brother finished in time.

Now, let's see. Where did I put that third sleeve?

chapter forty-one

it's time to **clean** your bedroom when . . .

Normal teenagers hate cleaning their rooms. Abnormal ones do, too—just ask me. In fact, as a teenager, I disliked cleaning so much that my bedroom was considered by the county as a nuclear-waste landfill. And that was *after* I'd tidied it.

When should you tackle your own hazardous site? When you notice any of these tell-tale clues:

• Flies, cruising within 10 feet of your dirty-clothes hamper, drop to the ground.

- The cupcake that rolled under your bed two months ago now has enough hair to French-braid.
- There's so much clutter on your floor that spiders have to walk on their hind legs just to get through.
- You open your closet door and get buried under more debris than Pompeii. (In fact, you've had so many closet avalanches the moths now wear hard hats.)
- The last time your sheets got washed was when you had a water balloon fight in bed.
- You can't walk barefoot on your floor without getting a paper cut.
- That glass of milk you left on your desk last week has turned green and is starting to bubble.
- There are enough potato chip crumbs in your bed to give a bed bug a blemish problem.
- The only thing hanging on your closet hangers are cobwebs.
- There's enough mold on the candy bar on your nightstand to provide a third-world country with penicillin for a year.
- The most recent store catalog in your room dates back to Thanksgiving—the first one.
- Your house gets robbed and the thief leaves a note in your room saying, "Don't blame this mess on me!"
- That stale pizza on your dresser is now doubling as a roach convention center.
- Your Michael W. Smith poster's even holding his nose.
- There are so many empty Coke cans on your floor the neighbors mistake your room for a recycling center.
- Your bed has seen more cookie crumbs than a Nabisco factory.

- You fluff your pillow and four bats fly out and thank you for releasing them.
- Archaeologists request permission to dig through the dust on your furniture in search of fossils.
- The health inspector demands hazard pay before checking out your bedroom.
- The only trash-free area in your room is the inside of your trash can.
- But you really know it's time to clean your bedroom when even your dirty socks get up and walk out!

a tan, like beauty, is only
skin deep

A lot of people spend the summer months working on their tans. I work on mine, too, but you can't tell. The Pillsbury Doughboy has more color in his arms and legs than I do in mine. In fact, if I want a tan line, I have to draw it with a felt marker.

Frankly, I don't understand how some people can get a tan under a flashlight with weak batteries while I'll lie on the beach for hours and all I'll get is rest.

I've tried everything to add a little color to my clown-white appearance. I've tried tanning creams, tanning butter, Sherwin-Williams paint, but nothing works. I've even tried going to tanning salons. But they just tell me I'm too late for the "Casper Look-Alike Contest" and send me home.

Once, in the ninth grade, I got desperate for a tan and tried some of that "instant tanning lotion." You know the stuff that promises to turn you into Malibu Barbie in just three to five hours? It didn't work, either. Oh, it gave me color. I turned such a bright shade of orange, I looked like I had taken a bath in Tang.

Orange, though, wasn't the color I was after. It clashed with my eyes and our school colors and wouldn't wash off. It had to *wear* off. So, I spent the next six weeks looking like a fluorescent emery board with feet. My friends loved it, though. They said with my new tangerine glow, I was a cinch to spot in the cafeteria line!

Recently, my son suggested I try spreading out aluminum foil on the beach, then lying on it.

"You really think that'd draw enough of the sun's rays to tan *my* body?" I asked him.

"Absolutely," he said. "'Course, you'd have to spread it from Los Angeles to San Francisco."

But that's all right. I know one of these days I'll get a good tan. One of these days I'll be able to lie on the beach without having aircraft complain about the glare. The next time a lifeguard yells "Great White! Great White!" I won't bow and say "Thank you! Thank you!" One of these days I'll look in the mirror and see that my skin has at last gotten some color. It will be that golden brown that I've dreamed of for so long.

Of course, with my luck, it'll just be because my freckles finally connected.

chapter forty-three

down to a **science**

Why I didn't receive a better grade in science is beyond me. I knew all about Sir Isaac Newton. (His fig cookies were my favorite.) I was quite familiar with the Law of Conservation of Energy, too. (My P.E. teacher said no one conserved energy as much as I did.) Still, most of what was taught in science class went right over my head.

For years I thought "The Big Dipper" was that burly guy

who worked at Baskin-Robbins. I didn't fully understand the principles of friction either. I knew I got it from my parents whenever I was on the telephone too long, but beyond that I was lost. And I couldn't tell you much about those dudes Plato, Aristotle, and Galileo, but I was pretty sure I had their latest album.

Frankly, I didn't see the need to study so much science. Why did I have to learn about electromagnetic waves? I didn't even surf. I didn't understand why I had to study Mars, either. Snickers was my favorite anyway. And why did I have to read about radioactivity? My radio was already active most of the time.

I also knew all I needed to know about genes: designer brands are the most expensive. I knew about fission, too. Before you drink your soda, you should wait for all the fission to stop. Or is that "fizzing"?

Working with the microscope was my least favorite thing to do in science. But that's understandable. After all, why would I want to look at creepy, crawling things under a microscopic lens when I could see all the creepy, crawling things I wanted to under my bed?

Then, there was our year-end project. It was worth a good portion of our grade, but no matter how hard I tried, I couldn't bring myself to do it. I'm referring, of course, to the dissection of a frog. I wanted no part of such an exercise. As far as I was concerned, I didn't need to see the insides of an amphibian . . . especially while he was still using them.

Luckily, though, the frog I got was the ticklish variety and took off hopping out the door the minute I touched him.

Don't get me wrong. I didn't fail science. The perfect score that I received on one of our assignments was just enough to pull me into the passing range. But I suppose I had an unfair advantage on that one. The assignment was to make fire and the teacher promised an "A" to the student who produced the very first flames. While the rest of the class worked like crazy rubbing two sticks together, I took my usual shortcut. I just used one of my recipes.

chapter forty-four

plug your **ears** with boughs of holly

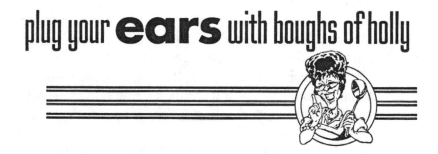

I love to go Christmas caroling. Singing, though, isn't one of my talents. I can get people to close their windows faster than a hurricane warning. When I go out caroling, even the snowmen cover their ears.

I used to carol every Christmas with our youth group. That is, until our youth pastor made me quit. He said my singing always got the neighborhood dogs to start howling and it'd throw him off key.

I believe he was being far too critical, though. After all, I was hitting the right notes. I wasn't hitting them in the right order, but I was getting to them eventually. Besides, had he forgotten about the time my voice actually broke crystal? Not the way it happens on that audio tape commercial, of course. I was just singing at a Sunday school banquet and the audience started throwing their glasses at me!

My singing presents special challenges for choir directors. Their biggest problem is figuring out where to place me. First, they try me out with the sopranos. Then, I'm placed with the tenors. Finally, they end up deciding I belong in the alto section . . . of another church!

I try not to let any of this get me down. I know I don't sing like Sandi Patti. I sound more like Carman. Okay, I sound more like Carman choking on some fettucini. But my voice does have a few positives. For one thing, it brings people together. Everyone agrees on how awful it is. My singing moves people, too. One year when I went caroling, 14 people put their houses up for sale.

So, you see, I've *got* to Christmas-carol every year. The real estate market depends on me. That's why last Christmas Eve I got out all my caroling books and decided to give it another try.

Looking back now, I shouldn't have. The lady at the first house didn't appreciate my rendition of "Jingle Bells" and went dashing through the snow just to get away from me. The man at the next house requested tapes. At first, I was flattered. Then, I realized he just meant adhesives so he could cover my mouth.

The last house, though, was the clincher. They turned out their lights, boarded up their windows, double-locked their doors, and stuffed cotton in their cat's ears. True, all the houses were doing that, but this one was especially insulting. And I told my family that when they finally let me in!

Brio

Designed especially for teen girls, *Brio* is packed with super stories, intriguing interviews and amusing articles on the topics they care about most—relationships, fitness, fashion and more—all from a Christian perspective.

All magazines are published monthly except where otherwise noted. For more information regarding these and other resources, please call Focus on the Family at (719) 531-5181, or write to us at Focus on the Family, Colorado Springs, CO 80995.